Magic Under the Willow Tree

Linda Bullock Haver

The Reading Glass
BOOKS

The Reading Glass Books
1-888-420-3050
www.readingglassbooks.com
production@readingglassbooks.com

Table of Contents

The inspiration for this
story came from the imagination
of my grandson Miles Haver. He was
playing with a kaleidoscope and wished
he could visit the different lands
that he pictured for each design.

Together Miles and I explored ideas
for storylines and characters.
He wanted the story
to have elements of mystery,
magic, problem solving,
and friendship.

Chapter 1

The Discovery

Oak and her brother Lock were concentrating so hard on their game of checkers that they didn't hear their mother call them the first two times. Oak had just declared her victory when their mother called up the stairs again. "Oakley Ann and Sherlock John, Dad and I are ready to go!"

"Hurry up, Lock," Oak told her younger brother. They both knew that when mom used their full names, she was getting annoyed.

They both scurried down the stairs and put on their shoes and sweatshirts.

"Did you forget we are going to the farm for lunch?" asked Mom.

"No," answered Lock. "We just lost track of time. We love going to Grandma and Grandpa

Wright's farm. We get to play with Maggie, run around outside and explore the barns. Let's go!"

When they pulled into the farm lane, Oak noticed Grandma and Grandpa rocking on the back porch. Maggie, the farm dog, ran to the car to greet Oak and Lock. Maggie was so glad to see them, she jumped up on Lock and gave him sloppy dog kisses. Then it was Oak's turn for Maggie's attention. Lock and Oak laughed so hard that they fell to the ground. Maggie looked sad when the kids went inside for lunch.

After lunch Oak and Lock played outside. They climbed trees, went on the tire swing, and rode bikes. They noticed Dad and Grandpa working on a project in the garage, so they went to ask them a question. "Can we explore the old barn next to the corncrib?"

"Of course, you can," Grandpa answered. "There's nothing very exciting in there, we just use it for storage. Take these flashlights with you, there is no electricity in that barn."

Flashlights in hand, Oak and Lock walked across the barnyard, past the biggest red barn to a smaller barn by the corn crib. When Lock slid open the barn door it made a loud squeaking sound. Oak thought the shadows in the barn made it look creepy. Then she turned on her flashlight, and it seemed much friendlier. They noticed old tools and horse harnesses hanging on one wall. There were stacks of tomato baskets and potato sacks piled high. Chicken feeders were stacked against the back wall. Some old farm equipment they didn't recognize sat in the center of the barn. It looked like nothing had been touched for years. They both decided that they didn't need to explore this barn anymore.

Just as they were about to leave, Lock noticed what looked like a door in the back corner of the barn. Lock unlatched the door and saw it was a tiny dark closet filled with pitchforks, shovels, buckets, and flowerpots. He was about to close the door when he noticed one of the floorboards in the front corner looked loose. Lock called for Oak to come and see what he had found.

Lock and Oak, who were both very curious, decided to pry up the floorboard to see what was there. They got an old hammer off the wall to help lift the board. Oak pointed her flashlight into the hole and was shocked to see a very old wooden box sitting in the dirt. Lock pulled the box out of the hole and set it on the floor. "Let's open it together," they both said at the same time. Before they opened the box, they each took one guess about what they would find. Lock guessed money and Oak guessed more tools.

Oak unlatched the box, and they lifted the lid. When they saw what was inside, they both had shocked looks on their faces. It looked like an old brass telescope. Oak picked it up and tried to look through it. "Lock, it's not a telescope, it's a kaleidoscope!"

They couldn't wait to show Mom, Dad, Grandma and Grandpa what they had found. The grown-ups were all sitting in the backyard. Lock and Oak ran over and showed them the kaleidoscope. The adults had puzzled looks on their faces when they realized what Oak was holding.

"Where did you find that wooden box?" asked Grandpa. "I've never seen it before," Grandma agreed.

Lock explained how they found it under a floorboard and then showed them the kaleidoscope inside the box.

"Wow," Dad added. "I played in all the barns when I was younger, and I never discovered a treasure like that one."

The adults all took turns looking into the kaleidoscope. They were very surprised to see how bright and clear the designs were after so many years of being forgotten.

"That must have been there when we bought this farm over fifty years ago," commented Grandpa. "I rarely go in the old closet in that barn, most of those things were in there when we moved to the farm. It seems like a very odd place to keep a kaleidoscope. There must be a story about why someone put in under the floorboards. The elderly couple who originally owned this farm didn't have any other family members so there is no one to ask for information. I guess this is a mystery that will never be solved."

Grandma added, "Oak and Lock, the kaleidoscope now belongs to the two of you according to our finders-keepers rule."

Oak and Lock both grinned. They were very excited to get the kaleidoscope cleaned up so they could show it to their friends. As always it had been a great day at the farm.

Chapter 2

The Surprise

The next day Oak and Lock decided to clean up their new treasure on the workbench in their garage. Mom gave them wood cleaner, brass polish, and several old rags. She explained the best way to do the job, then she got busy with her own work.

Lock wanted to start the cleaning with the brass on the kaleidoscope. He put a dab of polish on a rag and carefully rubbed it on the brass pieces. It started to shine immediately. When his hands got tired, Oak took over the job. In a few minutes the brass looked like new. They both thought it looked amazing on the outside. Oak let Lock take the first peek into the shiny eyepiece. He saw beautiful designs and patterns with colors that were bright and sparkling.

When he turned the object box at the end of the kaleidoscope (Oak had looked up what the parts of the kaleidoscope are called) the design morphed into many different ones. When Oak took her turn, she was amazed at what she saw.

They decided to clean the old wooden box next. It was in good shape, but very dirty and dusty. After they cleaned several layers of grime off the lid, Oak noticed some words etched into the center.

The Dazzling Dunes Magic Shop

Seaside Heights Boardwalk

New Jersey

They were surprised to learn that the kaleidoscope had been sold at a magic shop. Lock continued to clean the rest of the box to see if more information was hiding under the dirt. When Lock was wiping the inside bottom of the box, he noticed a tiny latch in one corner. "Look, I think there's a secret hiding place in the bottom of the box." When he pushed the latch, a false bottom popped up and they could see an old piece of paper lying there. Oak's hand was shaking as she pulled out the piece of paper.

"This is so exciting!" yelled Lock. "Read it out loud!"

Oak started to read…

How to Use the Magic Kaleidoscope

*Let the kaleidoscope's magic
take you on a quest*

You can visit other worlds as a guest

Each world will need a unique skill

Use it wisely and spread goodwill

Each design represents a magical land

Where the community needs a helping hand

Spin the kaleidoscope to a pattern you choose

Next the special magic words you should use

The land you choose will be colorful and bright

And you can do a good deed before it is night

*Even though in the new world
the day is very long*

*When you return to your home
no time will be gone*

Oak's voice got shakier with each word she read. "This has to be a joke, right?" she asked Lock. "Magic isn't real, is it?" Ten-year-old Oak was hoping seven-year-old Lock would have all the answers.

Lock was so excited he was jumping up and down. "I always thought magic could happen! Where are the magic words? I want to try it right now."

"Are you crazy?" Oak replied. "Give me time to think. Maybe we should do some research and see if the magic shop is still open so we can talk to someone who works there. Or maybe we should we talk to Mom and Dad and see what they think. But it would be amazing to visit a new world and do a good deed. Do you think this kaleidoscope can really be magical?"

While Oak was trying to figure out what to do next, Lock found the magic words and a warning on the back of the paper. He read them silently several times. He had already decided what he wanted to do. He just hoped his sister agreed.

<u>MAGIC WORDS FOR AN ADVENTURE</u>

This design I choose is beautiful and new

Take me to the world that is in my view

I accept this important quest

And promise to do my very best

<u>MAGIC WORDS TO GET HOME AGAIN</u>

Take me home

This adventure is done

I will be ready for the next one

Warning- these magic words will only work for <u>children</u> that have been chosen because they are kind to others, respectful of nature and are problem solvers.

Before Lock had time to share his plan with his sister, their mom called them into the house for lunch.

Oak and Lock were both grateful for some time to think about everything they had just discovered.

Chapter 3

The Decision

Oak and Lock were both very quiet at lunch. Oak was still thinking about what they should do next. Meanwhile, Lock already knew what he wanted to do, so he was thinking about how to get his sister to go along with his plan. After helping Mom clean up, Oak and Lock each went to their own room.

Lock picked up Dragon Breath who had been with him for as long as he could remember. Most kids' favorite stuffed animal is a teddy bear or a dog, but Lock's favorite stuffy and best friend was a lizard. Dragon Breath was a great listener, so Lock told him his plan. Lock knew Dragon Breath would agree his ideas were good (if he could talk). With Dragon Breath's silent approval, Lock was ready to present his plan to Oak.

Lock tapped on Oak's door and asked if he could come in to tell her his idea. Oak opened the door, still looking very confused.

Lock explained his plan. "I think we should take a chance and see if the kaleidoscope's magic really works. If it doesn't, we'll still own an amazing old kaleidoscope, but if it does, we could have an adventure we will never forget. The directions say we would be back home from the magical land before anyone misses us. I vote to give it a try. What do you think we should do?"

Oak's face relaxed and she smiled at Lock. "Okay, let's give it a try, I'm ready to go on a magical adventure."

Lock grabbed Dragon Breath out of his room, and they all headed to the garage. Oak picked up the wooden box, then they ran to their secret hiding place under the big willow tree in the backyard. The willow tree branches touched the ground and made the perfect place to try out the magic. Mom was busy pulling weeds in the flower garden and didn't even notice them.

"Why are you bringing Dragon Breath?" Oak asked Lock.

"I feel braver and stronger when I have him with me," answered Lock. "Plus, I've always told you that I think Dragon Breath has magical powers."

Oak just shook her head, rolled her eyes, and replied, "Whatever. Let's get started. We need to follow the exact directions very carefully."

Oak held her breath and spun the object box at the end of the kaleidoscope. When she peeked into the eyepiece, she saw a beautiful multicolored design. She held Lock's hand and together they said the magic words-

This design I choose is beautiful and new

Take me to the world that is in my view

I accept this important quest

And promise to do my very best

"Nothing's happening," said a disappointed Lock as they stood there looking at each other. "It doesn't work."

But just then they both heard a whooshing sound and a voice telling them, "You have to believe in the magic!" At that exact moment, Lock and Oak both realized it was Dragon Breath who was telling them to believe in magic. The next thing they remembered was a bright flash of light.

Chapter 4

The Journey

When the bright light faded Oak and Lock realized they were not in their backyard. "It worked!" yelled an excited Lock. "I wonder where we are."

Oak seemed liked she was still in a daze. She looked around with a confused look on her face and mumbled, "Ok, magic is real, now I do believe."

Dragon Breath started talking, taking the children by surprise. "Lock, you always believed I was magical, and you were right. I can speak when the magic around me is strong. We're in Balloon Land, and we must help solve a problem for the creatures that live here."

Oak and Lock looked around and were amazed that everything they saw was made of colorful balloons. Many shades of blue and white balloons made up the sky. The ground was made of green and brown balloons. Trees, bushes, and other plants were all different sizes of balloons.

Dragon Breath continued, "Balloon Land was created by a group of magical crickets who wanted to create a safe world for magical creatures. The weather here is aways perfect. It's never too hot or too cold. It's never windy, and it never has storms. The crickets wanted to make the best conditions for the balloons to last a long time so that all citizens could feel safe and happy."

Just then Lock pointed out some unicorns and a pegasus flying above their heads. He saw living rocks of all sizes with eyes that looked like they were guarding the land. Oak was shocked when she noticed green avocado like creatures running around helping others. These green creatures had legs, and eyes sticking up off their heads. Lock spotted what looked like tall colorful arrows with big eyes and long legs standing nearby.

"Balloon Land was always a happy place," Dragon Breath added. "I have many friends here and I want to help them. Everything was great until some balloons started popping. Each day more and more balloons are losing air and getting flat. If we can't solve this problem, Balloon Land will lose its magic and everyone that lives here will have to leave. Please find a way to help my friends."

Oak and Lock just looked at each other without saying anything. Of course they wanted to help Balloon Land, but they were just two human kids with a magical stuffed lizard. Could they help solve this mystery?

Chapter 5

Please Help

Just then Dragon Breath's friend Avo, one of the green avocado like creatures, came running up to Oak and Lock. It was hard not to stare, but Oak and Lock didn't want to be rude.

"You're here! You made it! Do you think you can help us?" Avo called out.

"We'll try our best," answered Lock. "If we all work together, we should be able to solve the problem."

Avo invited them to a special meeting at the community center where some of the creatures were gathering to problem solve. Oak, Lock, and Dragon Breath followed behind Avo as he led them to the meeting place. Oak and Lock both had trouble keeping their balance as they tried to keep up with Avo. The balloon ground was uneven and springy. It was like walking in a giant bounce house.

When they reached the meeting place, Oak peeked inside the building made of balloons. She noticed more balloons of every color used as furniture, walls, and decorations. It looked just like the colorful design they chose in the kaleidoscope.

It wasn't long before the community center was filled with the citizens of Balloon Land. Everyone seemed very worried. Avo introduced Oak and Lock to the crowd and slowly explained how the magic kaleidoscope had sent them to help. The crowd all cheered for Oak, Lock and Dragon Breath.

Dragon Breath spoke to the crowd. "We have one day to solve this mystery before the magic takes us home. Anyone with information about the balloons deflating, please share with us now."

A unicorn with pink stripes came forward and told them that the first balloons started popping about a month ago. A rainbow pegasus shared that she had collected several of the broken balloons so they could be checked out. One of the rock guards added that nothing suspicious had been noticed by any of the guards. One of the avocado creatures pointed out that many different new creatures including leprechauns, trolls, gnomes, sprites, and pixies moved to Balloon Land a few days before the balloons started popping. Oak and Lock knew all this information could be important pieces of the puzzle that they needed to solve, so they made sure to pay close attention.

Chapter 6

The Meadow

Oak thought the next step to solving the problem was to visit the crickets that created Balloon Land so they could see what the crickets had learned so far. Avo told them how to get to the meadow where the crickets lived. He also explained that the crickets were shy and liked to live alone so their chirping wouldn't bother the other citizens.

Oak, Lock, and Dragon Breath started on their walk to the meadow. They brought some of the broken balloons that Pegasus had found to show the crickets. After about half an hour they saw beautiful flowers covering the field ahead. When they got closer, they realized the flowers were different than anything they had ever seen. Each petal was made of a tiny colorful balloon.

Oak thought it was one of the most beautiful fields she had ever seen.

Lock noticed the meadow was just past the field, so they hurried to find the crickets. As they got closer, a very large yellow cricket with only two legs in the middle of his body hopped toward them. "Welcome friends," the cricket called out. "My name is Rocco, Avo sent me a message saying that you were coming. It's so nice to have visitors."

Rocco showed his new friends to a balloon house in the meadow. When they went in the house, they saw many other crickets of all shapes, colors, and sizes had come to help.

"We're very upset that Balloon Land is in danger," shared a cricket named Chad who was blue and had six enormous eyes. "We've been brainstorming but haven't come up with any solutions. Rocco and I helped create this land and we thought we had everything just perfect. Now this might be the end of Balloon Land."

Dragon Breath spoke up, "These are my friends Oak and Lock. They're not magical, but they were chosen by the magic kaleidoscope because they're very smart children and good problem solvers. I'm sure they can help."

Oak and Lock looked at each other and at the same time said, "We will do our best!"

Chapter 7

The Discussion

Oak started the discussion by asking the crickets to explain how they created Balloon Land.

Rocco spoke first. He told them the story of how Balloon Land was created. He shared that their first project was to come up with a way to control the weather so the balloons would last a long time. They couldn't use magic to make the weather perfect because they didn't have a spell that would last long enough. He told them Chad and a cricket named Brad from Flower Land came up with the idea to build a weather machine to keep the land at the perfect temperature, moisture level, wind speed, and air pressure for the balloons and our citizens.

Brad took the ideas back to Flower Land and built another weather machine there to make perfect weather for the flowers.

Chad shared that after the weather machine was finished, the crickets did many experiments to figure out the best way to make the balloons as strong as possible. They tried many thicknesses of different balloon materials to see what worked best. The decisions that were made were based on what was learned from the experiments.

"Now it seems like some big mistakes were made and Balloon Land is in trouble," Chad whimpered. He was so upset that he had tears streaming down from all six eyes.

The crickets shared that they had checked the weather machine and the broken balloons but couldn't find any problems.

Lock was quiet. He was listening carefully while the crickets were sharing their story. He had the beginning of an idea come to him. He concentrated on all the information and tried to put it together like the pieces of a puzzle. The more he concentrated the more he grinned. He leaned over and whispered to Dragon Breath. "I need to talk to Oak. I think I may have solved the mystery!"

Chapter 8

Good News

Lock was grinning from ear to ear when Oak and Dragon Breath joined him outside. Oak could tell from the look on Lock's face that he was about to tell them something very important. Lock took a deep breath and began to explain his excitement. "While I was listening to Rocco and Chad explain how they built Balloon Land, I kept getting this feeling that we were all missing a very important part of the puzzle. The crickets did an amazing job of using science to plan the perfect land. Everything was great for many years, but then slowly things started to change. Then I remembered that one of the avocado citizens told us that the changes started right after many new creatures moved to Balloon Land. Do either of you see the connection?"

Dragon Breath still had a confused look on his face, but Oak squealed with excitement and answered, "Yes, more creatures living here has changed the environment. The plans and experiments the crickets made for Balloon Land were based on the number of creatures living here when they built this magical land. Now that many more creatures have moved in the requirements need to be changed. The weather machine needs to be adjusted for the number of new citizens and the problem should be solved."

Oak, Lock, and Dragon Breath went back inside to share the good news with the crickets. Rocco and Chad were thrilled to hear their ideas and thought they made sense. They immediately started making plans to adjust the weather machine. The other crickets brainstormed ideas for ways to fix the damage that had already happened in Balloon Land.

Oak, Lock and Dragon Breath hurried back to the community center to let all the citizens know that the problem had been solved. The meeting turned into a party to celebrate the good news.

As the sun started setting, Oak, Lock, and Dragon Breath knew it was time for them to get back to the special place where the magic kaleidoscope had brought them to Balloon Land. As they walked along the path, they heard cheers of "Thank you!" and "Come visit anytime!"

They had just reached the magical place when the sun went down. Lock grabbed Oak's hand as he held Dragon Breath tightly to his chest. This time Dragon Breath did not have to remind them to believe in the magic. They said the magic words.

Take me home

This adventure is done

I will be ready for the next one

When they saw the bright light and heard the whooshing sound, they closed their eyes and hoped they were on their way home.

Chapter 9

Another Problem

When the whooshing sound stopped Oak and Lock opened their eyes. The sun was shining through the willow leaves and Mom was still weeding the flowers. They were back at home and only a few minutes had passed since they left.

Oak let out a sigh of relief and sat on the ground. Lock was so excited he danced around with Dragon Breath and chanted, "Magic is real, magic is real, and I was right!" Oak just smiled and didn't say a word.

They'd only rested a minute when the kaleidoscope started to glow. Oak and Lock had never seen that happen before. When they looked very closely, they noticed tiny letters that read, "We need you back in Balloon Land, NOW!"

Oak and Lock knew they had to follow the kaleidoscope's message. Their new friends needed their help. Lock grabbed Dragon Breath, then Oak's hand. Both kids said the magic words. When they opened their eyes, they were back in Balloon Land.

The first thing they saw was Avo running toward them. He was yelling, "We need you to travel to Flower Land to get Brad. Chad thought he fixed the weather machine, but it only worked for a few hours and now balloons are popping even faster than before, so he needs Brad's help."

"How can we travel to Flower Land?" asked Oak. "We don't know which design in the kaleidoscope will take us there."

"I can help you. I know the code design for Flower Land," answered Avo. "But only the children chosen by the kaleidoscope can use it to travel to different lands. Please hurry!"

Oak, Lock, and Dragon Breath held hands and said the magic words,

This design I choose is beautiful and new
Take me to the world that is in my view

I accept this important quest

And promise to do my very best

This time they opened their eyes to the amazing sight and smell of flowers. This had to be Flower Land.

Chapter 10

Flower Land

Dragon Breath spoke first. "I've been here many times. This is one of the most beautiful lands I've ever visited. There're so many flowers and colors here that can't be found anywhere else in the world."

Oak noticed a field of daisies, lilies, and irises ahead of them. "Look, the flowers are dancing like ballerinas. I love this place."

Lock was getting very annoyed. "Yes, the flowers are very pretty. But remember we're in a hurry. We need to move quickly."

Dragon Breath led them to a garden shed where he thought they would find Brad. A giant bee named Bumble met them at the door and asked, "Can I help you? I was just going out to collect some nectar. We had a problem with our weather machine last week and it snowed for about an hour. Luckily most of the flowers survived. Some of my bee friends and I are checking the nectar to see if the flowers are healthy. The crickets were able to fix the machine, so everything is back to normal."

"Yes, we need help. We're looking for a cricket named Brad," Lock answered. "Do you know where we can find him?"

"Sure," said Bumble. "Walk down the path past the ant farm. When you reach the beetle house, turn left. The cricket home is the first one on the right."

They knew they had reached the cricket home when they heard loud chirping. Lock knocked on the door. When the door opened a very large cricket told them Brad was resting in the garden behind the house. When he saw the visitors, Brad jumped up to greet them.

Dragon Breath quickly explained what was happening in Balloon Land and why they needed Brad to come with them.

"I'm happy to do what I can," said Brad. "You probably heard that we had a problem with our weather machine last week. While I was fixing our machine, I found a mistake that Chad and I made when we first made the machines. Several things had to be adjusted when more creatures moved here. I know exactly how to fix the problem. Let's go. I recently created a magical helicopter that we can use to quickly get to Balloon Land."

Soon after they flew to Balloon Land, Chad and Brad got to work on the weather machine. Brad taught Chad the way to adjust the machine, so it worked no matter how many creatures lived there. It took them about an hour to get it fixed. The balloons stopped popping and Balloon Land was saved.

Brad offered to fly Oak, Lock, and Dragon Breath home, but they decided to use the kaleidoscope. Oak was still shaking after riding in the speeding helicopter to Balloon Land.

Soon Oak, Lock, and Dragon Breath were safely back under the weeping willow tree in the back yard. When they peeked under the branches, they saw Mom was still working in the yard. She had not realized that they were gone!

A few minutes later, Mom called them to help her water the flowers. By the time the yard was cleaned up and all the tools were put away it was time for dinner.

As they were walking toward the house Mom told them she had a surprise. "Since today we had a quiet day at home and you didn't get to do anything exciting, Dad and I decided we should go to the beach tomorrow. We'll go to Island Beach State Park early tomorrow morning. We can take a picnic lunch and spend the day swimming, playing in the sand, and looking for shells."

Oak and Lock both smiled and thought to themselves that it'd be hard for a trip to the shore to beat the excitement of their day in Balloon Land and Flower Land.

Suddenly an idea popped into Oak's mind. "Mom, since we are going to Island Beach State Park, can we stop back to the Seaside Heights Boardwalk on our way home? We haven't been there for a long time, and it is right down the road from the park."

"I guess that would work," Mom answered. It might be fun to go to Seaside Heights Boardwalk for a change since we usually go to the boardwalk at Point Pleasant."

Lock couldn't wait to talk to Oak when they were finally alone. "You're a genius, Oak. I figured out why you asked if we could go to the Seaside Heights Boardwalk. While we're there, we can try to find out some information about the magic shop where the kaleidoscope came from. This is so exciting. We might be closer to solving the mystery of the wooden box and the magic kaleidoscope."

Chapter 11

Beach Day

The family left for the beach right after breakfast. Oak and Lock decided to play the alphabet game to help the hour ride go faster. Dad had just pulled the car into the street when Lock spotted acorns on the oak tree next door. "I see acorns for A," he shouted. The game moved quickly until they got to the middle of the alphabet. Oak got stuck on J for several minutes, then she noticed a girl jumping rope at a playground. Lock was sure he would have trouble finding something that started with Q but quickly spotted Queen Anne's Lace growing on the side of the road. The game continued until Dad pulled up to the gate to Island Beach State Park.

Everyone in the family had a great time at the swimming beach. The water was just the right temperature for body surfing, jumping waves, and riding boogie boards. Mom surprised them with her skills on a boogie board.

When they needed a break from the water, Oak and Lock joined other kids on the beach to build a huge sandcastle that held up well until high tide started coming in and knocking it down. While she was digging in the sand Oak found two shiny pieces of blue sea glass to add to her collection. Several of the kids found sand crabs then let them go in the water.

After a walk down the beach the whole family was ready for a late picnic lunch. When it was time to leave, they all went to the changing rooms to get dressed, then headed back to the car.

Oak and Lock had a great day at the beach but were excited about visiting the boardwalk. Mom and Dad thought the kid's excitement was about the rides, games, and junk food they were about to experience. But Oak and Lock couldn't stop thinking about their special magical kaleidoscope. Could the magic shop still be there? Would anyone be able to give them more information? There were so many questions they needed to ask before this mystery could be solved.

Chapter 12

The Boardwalk

Dad pulled into an empty parking spot near the boardwalk. The family's first stop was at the Balloon Pop Water Race. Mom, Dad, Lock, and Oak lined up with their water guns ready to go. At the sound of the bell the race started. Dad had the lead for a few seconds, then Mom went ahead. At the last second Oak raced past Mom and won the game. Oak's prize was a small stuffed dog.

Next the family went into an arcade. Mom and Dad played several games of Skee-Ball while Oak and Lock tried a couple of the driving challenges. Then they all tried a few more games before they decided it was time for dinner.

After pizza at their favorite boardwalk restaurant, Mom and Dad told Oak and Lock they could each get tickets for two of the rides. Oak loved spinning rides and Lock loved rollercoasters. When the rides were done, they decided to find a nice bench where they could sit and watch the ocean. After a few minutes, Oak asked her parents if Lock could go with her to the candy shop right behind them. She wanted to get a bag of caramel corn for everyone to share. Mom and Dad were tired, so they stayed on the bench and watched the kids go in the candy shop.

As soon as they got in the shop Oak asked the store owner, who was behind the counter, if he knew anything about a magic shop that was on the boardwalk many years ago. The man smiled and said, "This is your lucky day. This is the building that was a magic shop before my family bought it when I was just a boy. When my dad was fixing up the building, he found a flyer from the magic shop behind a wall. He thought it was so interesting that he framed it and hung it up. It was hanging here for many years until we remodeled the store a few years ago. Would you like to see it? I still have it on a shelf in the back room."

Oak and Lock both answered, "Yes" at the same time. The man got the framed flyer and laid it on the counter. When Oak and Lock read the flyer, they had trouble hiding their excitement. The man told them he had made several copies of the flyer and asked them if they would like one. Oak read the flyer out loud.

Professor Morwen Wraithbane

Dares You to Enter

The Dazzling Dunes

Magic Shop

Get ready for a magical adventure

into a world of wonder and enchantment

located on the Seaside Heights Boardwalk

near the Fun House

"Now we know the name of the man who owned the magic shop," said Lock. "I bet we can find out more information about him on the internet."

Oak and Lock thanked the store owner and were about to walk out of the door when they remembered they told Mom and Dad they would buy caramel corn.

The family enjoyed the bag of caramel corn in the car on the way home. Even though it was one of Oak and Lock's favorite treats, they hardly ate any because they were too excited.

Would this new information help them learn more about their magical kaleidoscope?

Chapter 13

More Mystery

The next morning Oak and Lock researched the mysterious Professor Morwen Wraithbane on Mom's computer. Oak told Mom the professor was a character in a book she read, and she wanted to see if he was a real person. Oak was very disappointed when she couldn't find out any more about the kaleidoscope or Professor Wraithbane. Lock thought that maybe Dragon Breath could give them more information the next time he had his magical powers. That gave Lock the idea to ask their parents where Dragon Breath came from. Maybe his stuffed lizard was the key to another clue.

Oak and Lock found Mom in the kitchen making cookies. "It smells so good in here. Can we have a cookie?" asked Lock.

Mom handed them each a warm, gooey chocolate chip cookie and a glass of milk. "I knew the smell of fresh baked cookies would get you both to the kitchen," said Mom. "Now you can help me out with a couple of things."

After their snack Oak took the towels out of the dryer and folded them while Lock helped Mom clean up the cookie making dishes. Oak heard Lock ask Mom, "Who gave me Dragon Breath? He's my favorite stuffy and I don't know how I got him."

Mom smiled and answered, "It's a mysterious story. After you were born, we got a package in the mail that was addressed to Sherlock John. When we opened it, Dragon Breath was inside. There was no card attached and no return address. We thought it must be from one of Dad's clients, but none of them ever mentioned sending the package. So, we never found out who it was from. Dragon Breath was your special friend from the first time you held him." Lock was glad Mom told him the story of getting Dragon Breath, but he still had so many questions.

When they were done with their chores, Oak and Lock met under the willow tree. Lock told Oak the story Mom shared with him about getting Dragon Breath. "I think we should plan to go on another magical adventure using the kaleidoscope," Oak said after hearing the story. "Dragon Breath may have some answers for us, and we may be able to help another magical community."

"I think that's a great idea," Lock replied. "Let's go tomorrow. Dad will be at work and Mom has her book club meeting here, so she'll want us to play outside."

Oak agreed. Tomorrow they'd use the kaleidoscope to go on their second magical journey.

Chapter 14

Another Adventure

In the morning Oak and Lock helped Mom get ready for her book club meeting. When everything was done and Mom's friends were starting to arrive, Mom told them they could play outside.

Oak went to get the kaleidoscope box, and Lock grabbed Dragon Breath. They met under the willow tree. This time it was Lock's turn to spin the object box at the end of the kaleidoscope. After a few spins, he decided to stop on a design with many shades of green and blue. Oak and Lock were much less nervous this time. They both tried to picture where the journey would take them. Then they held hands and repeated the magic words.

This design I choose is beautiful and new
Take me to the world that is in my view
I accept this important quest
And promise to do my very best

When the bright light dimmed, they opened their eyes to see a beautiful lake filled with lily pads and surrounded by tall trees. "The colors are exactly like the design I chose in the kaleidoscope," whispered Lock. "Where do you think we are?"

Dragon Breath answered, "I've been here before. This is Frog Land. There are magical frogs of all sizes, shapes, and colors from all over the world living here. Something must be wrong. Usually, it's very noisy with all the croaking, ribbitting, peeping, and bellowing from so many different types of frogs."

"You're right," said a giant frog hopping up behind them. "There is a big problem in Frog Land. We think the lake is making us sick. The little frogs are so ill they can't eat, and the tadpoles are lying very still under the water instead of swimming around. I don't know how much longer they can last. Some of the bigger frogs have lost their ability to speak and are having trouble hopping. Even the giant frogs like me are starting to suffer."

"Hello, Biggy Green," Dragon Breath said to the giant frog. "Sorry to hear your land is having trouble. These are my friends Oak and Lock. The kaleidoscope brought us here to see if we can help."

"Thank goodness," replied Biggy Green. "We think we know what is wrong, but we don't know how to solve the problem. A new type of weed started growing in the lake about a month ago. It's a very pretty plant, so we just let it grow. It spread very quickly. By the time we realized it was changing the water it was too late. We can't figure out how to get the plant out of the lake. We tried to use our magic but that only made the weed grow faster. When we pulled it out it grew back thicker.

We know there is a laboratory for magical scientists in a town about 10 miles from here that would have someone who could help us. But our magic only works in our land, and it's too far away for a sick frog to hop there."

"That must be the reason why the kaleidoscope sent us here," said Oak. "We can travel to the neighboring land to get help. Just tell us the way."

Biggy Green drew them a detailed map and they started on their journey.

Chapter 15

A Different Journey

To get to the magic laboratory, Oak and Lock had to walk around the lake, over three big hills and down into a valley.

While walking around the lake they saw more varieties of frogs than they had ever seen before. Some of the frogs were so tiny they looked like bugs. Some were bigger than Biggy Green. One was almost as tall as Lock. They saw frogs with stripes, polka-dots, and plaid. There were pink, blue, purple, and orange frogs. They saw several frogs with six eyes, some medium sized frogs with eight legs, and tadpoles that were gold and silver.

When they made it around the lake, Lock spoke up, "That was amazing. I never knew there could be so many kinds of frogs."

"You should've seen Frog Land when all the frogs were healthy," Dragon Breath shared. "There were so many frogs hopping around that you had to be careful where you walked. Also, the noise they made was so loud you had to yell when you talked. I hope we can get the scientists to help them so Frog Land can get back to normal."

Luckily the first hill they came to was not too steep, so the climb up and down was easy. The next hill was a little more challenging, but they made it over without a rest. However, they were huffing and puffing after climbing the third hill. When they all sat down for a rest, Lock noticed a building in the valley ahead of them. "That must be where the laboratory is located. We're almost there!" he shouted. "Let's go."

Chapter 16

The Magic Laboratory

When they reached the laboratory, Oak used the giant door knocker to let the scientists know that someone was there. When the door opened, Oak and Lock were both shocked to see the man standing there had the head of an octopus and eight arms covered in fish scales. "Hello, how can I help you?" asked the man.

Dragon Breath spoke first. "Hello, Doctor Aquatic. I don't know if you remember me. I am Dragon Breath, and we met many years ago when I visited the lab with Professor Morwen Wraithbane. My friends and I have come to ask for help for Frog Land. Their lake is changing and hurting the frogs. They think a new type of weed growing in the water is causing the problem. The frogs all need your help."

"Everyone follow me," said Doctor Aquatic. "Let's get the other scientists on my team to join us and you can tell us exactly what is happening in Frog Land."

While they were walking down the hall, Lock gave Dragon Breath a puzzled look and asked, "Why didn't you tell us about Professor Morwen Wraithbane when you could talk in Balloon Land?" Oak and I just found out he owned the magic shop where the kaleidoscope came from."

"My magic is limited," explained Dragon Breath. "I can never share new information with anyone. I can only explain information they already know. Now that you know about the Professor, I can answer any of your questions. But now we need to focus on getting help for Frog Land. Time is running out for them."

Dr Aquatic led Oak, Lock, and Dragon Breath through the door to the magical laboratory. The room was beyond anything they could have imagined. There were bubbling beakers and test tubes filled with liquids of every color. Plants and small animals were floating in the air. The ceiling looked exactly like the sky with clouds moving around. Water was flowing like a river in the middle of the room. Even Dragon Breath was amazed at everything he saw.

Before Oak and Lock had time to ask questions, two more scientists came over to talk to them. "These are the other scientists on my team," explained Doctor Aquatic, "Doctor Terra Mater and Doctor Hera. Can you guess which one deals with magic on the land and which one deals with magic in the air?"

Lock answered, "I guess the scientist with grass for hair and rocks for shoulders is the one that takes care of magic on Earth. She must be Doctor Terra Mater, named after the Roman Goddess of Earth. Doctor Hera must be named after the Greek goddess of air. The feathered wings and arms were another clue that she deals with magic in the air."

Doctor Aquatic laughed, "You're right. And of course, I deal with magic in the water. How did you know all that information, Lock?"

Lock giggled and quickly answered, "Dragon Breath whispered it to me."

Oak and Lock took turns telling the scientists what was happening in Frog Land. Dragon Breath filled in the details they forgot.

"You came to the right place. This problem should be easy to fix," said Doctor Aquatic. "These kinds of problems are our specialty. Now let's hurry to Frog Land."

Chapter 17

Saving Frog Land

Doctor Terra Mater used her magic to help the group travel quickly to Frog Land. Biggy Green met them under a tree by the lake.

"Thanks for coming," Biggy Green told the scientists. "Every day we all get sicker and weaker."

All three scientists quickly got to work. Doctor Aquatic dove in the lake to get specimens from the water and the plants growing there. Doctor Hera used her wings to check the air quality and wind direction. Doctor Terra Mater inspected the quality of the dirt and the plants growing around the lake. Oak and Lock were tingling from all the magic in the air.

When their work was done, the three scientists got together to discuss their findings. Doctor Aquatic spoke first. "You were right Biggy Green.

The lake is being poisoned by the new weed that's growing so quickly, but don't worry we came up with a plan to get rid of it."

"We know the weed comes from an enchanted land east of Frog Land," added Doctor Hera. "We think seeds are accidently getting stuck to birds that live in the enchanted land. When those birds fly over Frog Land the seeds are dropped into your lake. We're sure it was just bad luck, and no one planned for this to happen."

Doctor Terra Mater was busy creating the potions needed while her teammates were talking. "Everything is ready," she explained. "Let's get started saving Frog Land."

The three scientists used the potions and special magic spells to rid the lake of the dangerous weeds. Oak and Lock were surprised to see how quickly the weeds in the lake disappeared. One of the potions instantly made all the frogs and tadpoles healthy again. A great cheer came from all around. The scientists had saved them.

After many croaks of thanks, the scientists traveled back to their lab. Oak, Lock, and Dragon Breath made their way back to the place where the kaleidoscope first brought them to Frog Land.

While they were walking a flock of big birds flew over their heads. Lock started to look worried. "Those birds made me think of something important. I'm glad the scientists solved the weed problem but if birds are always flying over Frog Land couldn't it happen again? We can't go home yet. Frog Land still needs our help."

Chapter 18

Dragon Breath's Idea

Lock, Oak, and Dragon Breath turned around and hurried back to the lake. Biggy Green saw them coming and ran to meet them.

"I just realized that your problems may not be over," Lock said. Then he explained to Biggy Green that as long as the birds from the enchanted land were flying over Frog Land the weeds could keep coming back.

"I can't believe we never thought about that possibility," sighed Biggy Green. "What can we do? We don't want to hurt the birds. Should we get the scientists to come back to help?"

Dragon Breath answered, "I think we need to travel to the enchanted land of Crystal Hollow where the birds live. King Cornelius, who rules that land, has very powerful magic and may be able to solve this problem so it never happens again, and no one gets hurt."

Oak and Lock agreed with Dragon Breath. "I'll travel with you," said Biggy Green. "Now that I'm healthy, I can make the trip. Crystal Hollow is in the east and not very far away. Let me tell my family and then we can get started."

Chapter 19

Crystal Hollow

When the friends entered the valley where Crystal Hollow was located, they were amazed at what they saw. The mountains on both sides of the valley were covered with crystalized rocks of blue, purple, and red. The sun made the crystals shine like diamonds. The king's gem covered castle sparkled in the middle of the valley. Even the streetlights gleamed and twinkled like little stars.

Biggy Green called out to the guard near the entrance to Crystal Hollow. "We're here to see King Cornelius. Frog Land needs his help."

The guard answered, "The king is always happy to meet with citizens of other lands. I'll let him know you're coming."

On the walk to the castle Oak kept pointing out more sparkling things along the path. "Look, the sidewalks are crystalized glass. The leaves on the trees glow in the light. This place is beyond imagination."

When the friends reached the castle, the door magically opened and said, "Welcome to Crystal Hollow. The king will see you now. Follow the shining star in front of you and it will lead the way."

The star led them to the throne room where the king was sitting on a jewel covered chair. "Come in and sit down," he said. "Tell me how I can help you."

Biggy Green and Dragon Breath took turns telling the king about the problem in Frog Land. Oak and Lock stood very quietly because they were both shy being around a king.

Oak whispered very softly to Lock, "Do you think we'll ever get used to visiting all these magical lands?" Lock just shrugged his shoulders.

The king listened very carefully to everything Biggy Green and Dragon Breath shared, then said, "Let me talk to my advisors. I'm sure we can solve this problem. No land should have to suffer if there is something we can do to help. While I'm having my meeting go to the dining room and enjoy the snacks my cook has made."

Oak, Lock, Dragon Breath, and Biggy Green found their way to the dining room. They sat down at a large table filled with cookies and cakes. They were not surprised to see that even these treats were glittery and sparkling.

Several minutes later King Cornelius joined them in the dining room. "We've come up with a plan that should make everyone happy," the king shared. "I'll make a magical invisible dome over Frog Land. It'll protect your land from birds dropping seeds and the birds will still have the freedom to fly wherever they want. The dome will be open at the bottom so that the frog community and their visitors can travel in and out whenever they want. Do you agree that this plan will solve the problem?"

Oak, Lock, Dragon Breath, and Biggy Green all thought that it was a great plan. It would stop any future problems with seeds falling in the lake.

"I'll travel to Frog Land right now in my magical carriage," said the king. "Please join me."

Outside the castle a carriage that was glistening like a thousand little lights was waiting for them. As soon as they all got into the carriage it magically flew into the sky. Oak realized she was holding her breath, not because she was afraid but because she couldn't believe what was happening.

The trip to Frog Land only took a few seconds. When they landed, King Cornelius greeted the frog community and told them about his plan. The frogs cheered as the king used his magical powers and placed a dome over Frog Land. The dome was invisible but made the sky sparkle in the sunlight. Now Frog Land looked even more magical. The king encouraged the frogs to come to his enchanted land anytime they needed help. Then the king returned to Crystal Hollow in his carriage.

Oak, Lock, and Dragon Breath said a second good-bye to their friends in Frog Land, then hurried back to the spot where the kaleidoscope would bring them home.

Chapter 20

Questions and Answers

When they reached the spot that would take them home Lock suggested that they take some time for Dragon Breath to tell them more about Professor Morwen Wraithbane.

Before Dragon Breath had time to say anything a voice behind them yelled, "Oak, Lock, I'll tell you anything you want to know."

Oak and Lock turned around and saw a short, thin man in flowing robes walking toward them. Who was this stranger and how did he know their names?

"Hello children, I'm Professor Morwen Wraithbane," shared the stranger. "I know you have many questions for me. Please don't be upset with Dragon Breath. He was following my directions. I'm so happy to meet you. Both of you have been very helpful to the magic community."

"We are excited to help," Oak said, "but we need to know why all this is happening."

The Professor smiled and answered, "Dragon Breath has been keeping me up to date on your adventures. Let me tell you a story that may answer many of your questions and will help you better understand how you became part of my story."

"Many, many years ago when I was a boy," the professor started, "my father gave me the same kaleidoscope that now belongs to both of you. He saw it at a magic shop in London and knew I would like it. I was fascinated by the beautiful colored designs but had no idea it was magical. When I found the directions that came with the kaleidoscope, I started on magical adventures just like the two of you. On one of my journeys, I visited the land of stuffed animals. That's where I met Dragon Breath. We became best friends and traveled to magical places around the world. When I grew up, I no longer needed the kaleidoscope because I had learned to do magic on my own.

Then Dragon Breath and I moved to the United States for a new adventure, and I opened the Dazzling Dunes Magic Shop on the boardwalk. It was fun meeting new people and teaching them magic tricks. I kept the kaleidoscope under the counter because I was waiting for the right child to visit the shop so I could give it to them. But years went by and there was never a child that seemed just right to receive my gift.

One day Dragon Breath came up with a great idea. We should let the kaleidoscope choose the child. The kaleidoscope led us to an old farm with many outbuildings. We picked one of the barns and buried the kaleidoscope under the floorboards in a small closet."

"I know what happened next," said Lock. "Oak and I found the kaleidoscope."

"You're correct," said the professor. "Let me catch my breath then I will tell you the rest of the story."

The professor closed his eyes and quickly fell asleep.

Chapter 21

The Story Continues

"Professor Wraithbane is very old and tires very easily," Dragon Breath told Oak and Lock. "So, I'll tell you the rest of the story. Even when the kaleidoscope was buried, its magic was still very strong. The professor could feel its magic over the years.

Before you were born, he knew that you were the children that would find the kaleidoscope. It was my idea for the professor to send me as a gift to Lock when he was a baby. When you started your magical adventures, I wanted to be there to help you."

Oak and Lock were surprised and shocked to hear everything the professor and Dragon Breath had told them.

Oak was the first one to speak. "I never believed magic was real until our adventure to Balloon Land. Now we find out that we were chosen to be part of this magical story. That's a lot of responsibility."

Lock agreed with Oak. He looked at Dragon Breath with a big grin and said, "All those times I pretended that you were magical and could take me on adventures around the world, I never truly believed it could happen."

Professor Wraithbane opened his eyes and yawned loudly. "I see Dragon Breath finished the story for me. It's getting late. You children need to get back home. You'll meet me again someday in another magical land."

Oak, Lock, and Dragon Breath held hands and said the magic words.

Take me home

This adventure is done

I will be ready for the next one

Chapter 22

A New Beginning

Oak, Lock, and Dragon Breath were magically back under the willow tree in their yard. They could hear their mom and her friends chatting in the house.

"I need to go to my room and think about everything that just happened," said Oak. "Right now, it all seems like a dream. Can you believe we rode in a magical helicopter and carriage? We now have frog friends and know amazing scientists. Could you ever have imagined a land made of balloons? We got to visit an enchanted land and meet a king. What other adventures could possibly be in our future?"

Lock agreed with Oak that they never could've dreamed all the things they'd experienced. "I have an idea," Lock replied. "Let's go on one more adventure tomorrow. School starts on Monday, so it'll be harder use the kaleidoscope when we are busy during the week." Oak liked Lock's idea.

Lock and Dragon Breath headed up to their room too. "I wish you could always answer when I talked to you," Lock said to Dragon Breath. "Did you just wink at me?" Lock continued, "or am I just very tired?"

After her book club friends went home, Mom asked Oak and Lock if they wanted to play a board game with her. They had a great time munching on the leftover book club snacks and playing Chutes and Ladders. "I'm sorry that you two had to play by yourselves so much this summer," said Mom. "It was a very busy time with Dad working so much. We didn't get to go on many fun trips."

"Don't worry, Mom," said Oak. "I'm sure Lock and I'll have many adventures in the future."

Oak and Lock looked at each other and grinned.

Chapter 23

Help Needed

The next morning after breakfast Oak and Lock, who was holding Dragon Breath, met under the willow tree. Oak was getting ready to turn the kaleidoscope to choose a design when it started to vibrate and glow. This time the message read "Help needed in Stuffy Land, come quickly." The kaleidoscope began to magically turn by itself to the correct design for Stuffy Land. Oak and Lock held hands and said the magic words. When they opened their eyes, they knew they were in Dragon Breath's old homeland. Everything there looked soft, squishy, and cuddly.

Dragon Breath had tears in his eyes as he looked around and said, "I forgot how much I missed my first home. I hope some of my friends are still here."

Just then, they heard someone in the bushes whisper, "Dragon Breath, it's me your friend Diego Dog. Larry Lamb and I sent the message to the kaleidoscope. We're hiding in the bushes, so Toy Master won't find us. You and your friends should meet us in our old tree house, then we'll tell you exactly what's going on."

Dragon Breath led Oak and Lock to an old tree house in the forest. When they climbed the ladder, they found Diego and Larry waiting for them.

"We're safe here," said Larry. "Diego and I are the only stuffies left that know about this tree house."

"Who is Toy Master and why do you need to hide from him?" asked Oak.

"It all started about a month ago," Diego started. "Toy Master, who is half human and half stuffy bunny, came to Stuffy Land to ask for help. He told us everyone in his land was making fun of him because a wizard had put a curse on him and made him half stuffy. He asked if he could live with us. He brought a few stuffed animals with him. Their names are Peggy Pig, Harvey Horse, and Wally Wombat."

Larry continued the story, "At first everything was great. It was nice to have some new friends to play with. Then one day we couldn't find Gerry Giraffe anywhere. The next day Elmer Elephant and Lucy Lion were missing. Since then, more stuffies have disappeared. That's when Diego and I decided to investigate the mystery of the missing stuffies. We hid behind Toy Master's house. Then we heard him telling his stuffies Peggy, Harvey, and Wally to find more stuffy friends to trick into coming with them. The Toy Master wants to take all the stuffies to Sorcerer's Spire where the wizard lives."

"That's when we found out that the Toy Master and his stuffies came to our land to capture us and take us to work for an evil wizard," added Diego. "That's also when we decided to send you the message that we needed help."

"I'm glad you asked us to come here," Oak said. "If we all work together, I'm sure we can come up with a plan to save the stuffies." Lock and Dragon Breath nodded in agreement.

Chapter 24

The Plan

"I've been thinking," said Lock, "Stuffed animals are usually sweet, cuddly, and help make you feel good. Peggy, Harvey, and Wally are just the opposite of most stuffies. Maybe they are following Toy Master's directions and are acting strange because they are under a spell. If we can get them away from Toy Master's magic maybe they can help us defeat Toy Master and save the missing stuffed animals."

"It'll be tricky to get Peggy, Harvey, and Wally alone," added Diego. "Toy Master needs them to stay very close to him."

Dragon Breath added to the plan. "I have an idea. How about if I pretend to be the wizard's helper stuffy that was sent to give them a message? I could wait until Toy Master takes his afternoon nap, then get Peggy, Harvey, and Wally to come with me to the forest so I can talk to them alone. I know about their plan so they can't trick me. Then, hopefully I can convince them to help us." Everyone thought it was a good plan.

"Let's give it a try," said Larry. "Don't worry Dragon Breath. We'll all be hiding in the forest if you need help. We will not let Toy Master capture another stuffed animal."

Chapter 25

The Spell is Broken

Diego told Dragon Breath that Toy Master took a nap in the hammock behind his house every day at 1:00 pm. At 1:08 pm Dragon Breath quietly tiptoed into Toy Master's backyard. He noticed Peggy, Harvey and Wally sitting by a tree next to the hammock where Toy Master was snoring loudly. The three stuffies looked up and saw Dragon Breath coming into the yard. They ran over and asked, "Who are you? We've never seen you here before. What do you want?"

Dragon Breath told them, "The wizard sent me to give Toy Master and the three of you a message. I'm one of his assistants. I don't want to wake Toy Master right now so let's go to the forest and I'll give you all the details of the message. I can talk to Toy Master later."

Peggy, Harvey, and Wally followed Dragon Breath into the forest because they were anxious to hear what the wizard wanted. Dragon Breath stopped when he got to the place where he knew his friends were hiding behind the trees.

"Please listen to me very carefully," Dragon Breath said to Peggy, Harvey, and Wally. "I think Toy Master put all three of you under a spell so you would follow his directions. I don't think stuffed animals like you would choose to be mean and trick other stuffies. I think Toy Master makes you do bad things. I had to get you far away from him to break the spell."

At first the three stuffies looked confused and puzzled. Then Peggy spoke up, "I think Dragon Breath might be right, lately everything I do seems like I'm in a dream. Now I remember it all started when the three of us were called to Sorcerer's Spire where the wizard was waiting for us. I don't remember anything else until just now when I realized we were in the forest."

"You are right Peggy," Harvey and Wally said at the same time. "Now we remember too."

Diego, Larry, Oak, and Lock came out of their hiding spots to join Dragon Breath.

"Now that you are no longer under the spell of Toy Master, we can tell you the whole story," shared Larry. "Toy Master made you trick our stuffy friends and now they have disappeared. We hope you can help us get them back home."

"Sure", Harvey said. "We will…

Before Harvey could finish his sentence, Toy Master ran into the forest yelling, "All of you stay right where you are!"

Chapter 26

A Rescue

Oak, Lock, and all the stuffed animals were surprised and too scared to move as Toy Master hurried toward them. They were afraid Toy Master would cast a new spell on everyone.

"Please don't be scared," said Toy Master. "I was standing at the edge of the forest, and I heard everything. You're right Dragon Breath. Peggy, Harvey, and Wally were under a spell, not from me, but from the wizard. He tricked all of us into doing his work. I tried to resist and that's when he turned me into half stuffy. I love stuffed animals and would never hurt them."

"What was the wizard's plan?" asked Lock. "Where are the missing stuffies and why did the wizard need them?"

Toy Master answered with a sigh, "Our job was to capture all the citizens of Stuffy Land and take them to Sorcerer's Spire. Then the wizard would put them all under his spell so he would have an army of stuffies to help him take over other lands.

The wizard dreams of ruling over all the magical world. He wants to use his powers to trick others and change every magical creature. His plan is to stop all magic except his.

The good news is the stuffies we captured are still here. We have them in a cave on the other side of the forest. We're supposed to deliver them to the wizard in two days."

"I have an idea about what we can do to trick the wizard," said Oak. "Let's go rescue the stuffies from the cave. Then I'll explain my plan to everyone."

Oak, Lock, and the stuffies followed Toy Master to the cave. The captured stuffies were afraid when they saw Toy Master, Peggy, Harvey, and Wally. Diego, Larry, and Dragon Breath told them the whole story and convinced them they were safe now.

Oak shared her plan with her new friends and all the stuffies from the cave.

Gerry Giraffe spoke up, "Of course we'll help anyway we can. We need to do everything possible to stop the wizard from taking over." A big cheer came from the stuffies as they all agreed with Gerry.

Chapter 27

Oak's Idea

Oak explained her idea for tricking the wizard. All the stuffed animals and Toy Master would travel to Sorcerer's Spire. They would pretend to be under the spell of the wizard so the wizard would trust them. Oak and Lock would use the kaleidoscope to go visit the magic laboratory to ask the scientists to make them a magic potion to change the bad wizard into a good one.

Then Oak and Lock would go to Sorcerer's Spire with the potion. Toy Master and all the stuffies would pretend that Oak and Lock were children that wanted to help the wizard with his plan to rule over all the lands. Dragon Breath would pour the potion into the wizard's drink and their problem would be solved.

"Do you really think the plan will work?" asked Dragon Breath.

"There is only one way to find out," added Toy Master. "We need to get started now."

Chapter 28

Celebration

So far Oak's plan was working. The stuffies and Toy Master did a great job of pretending they were under the wizard's spell. The wizard was fooled and shared all his ideas for taking over the magical lands. He even made Dragon Breath his special helper.

Oak and Lock were welcomed back to the magic laboratory and the scientists were happy to make a potion to change the wizard.

When Oak and Lock reached the Sorcerer's Spire with the potion, Gerry Giraffe opened the door to let them in. Dragon Breath quickly took the potion and hid it in the kitchen. Toy Master introduced the children to the wizard and convinced him Oak and Lock wanted to work for him.

"Why would you children want to help me?" asked the wizard.

Lock answered for them, "Our parents are very mean to us, and we are unhappy and angry. We never had a friend until we met Toy Master. He told us about your plan, and we want to help you take over the other lands. We want to be powerful too." Oak was surprised to see that Lock was such a good actor.

"Children will be very helpful," said the wizard. "Toy Master, you did a good job finding this girl and boy to help me accomplish my dream."

Just then Dragon Breath walked in carrying a tray of glasses filled with lemonade. The wizard's special fancy glass was up front. Dragon Breath announced it was time to celebrate the wizard's plan. Everyone took a glass and held it in the air to cheer the wizard.

After he took a large gulp from his special glass, the wizard blinked his eyes several times, then he looked around the room in surprise. "Why is everyone here? Is this a party for me? Where did all these stuffed animals come from? I love stuffies!" The potion had worked!

Then the real celebration started. The Toy Master promised to take the stuffies back to their land. He asked if he could stay with them and live in Stuffy Land. Every stuffy yelled, "Yes." Some of the stuffies decided to stay at Sorcerer's Spire and help the good wizard do good deeds throughout the land.

Oak, Lock, and Dragon Breath realized they should be getting home. They said good-bye to all their new friends. Dragon Breath had the hardest time saying good-bye to his old friends Diego and Larry, so he promised he would try to visit again soon.

When they got to a wooded area, Oak pulled the kaleidoscope out of her backpack. They held hands and said the magic words to go home.

Take me home

This adventure is done

I will be waiting for the next one

When they opened their eyes, they were back under the willow tree. It wasn't even a second before they heard another swooshing sound and the kaleidoscope lit up. The message read, "It's Professor Wraithbane…HELP!"

It was at that moment that Oak and Lock knew this wouldn't be their last adventure.